FOX AND HIS FRIENDS

by Edward Marshall

pictures by James Marshall

THE DIAL PRESS NEW YORK

Dial easy-to-read

For Christian and Juretta

Published by
The Dial Press
1 Dag Hammarskjold Plaza
New York, New York 10017

Text copyright © 1982 by Edward Marshall
Pictures copyright © 1982 by James Marshall
All rights reserved. Manufactured in the U.S.A.
First printing

Library of Congress Cataloging in Publication Data
Marshall, Edward. Fox and his friends.
Summary: In three separate episodes Fox wants to play
with his friends, but duty in one form or another interferes.
[1. Foxes—Fiction. 2. Humorous stories]
I. Marshall, James, 1942– ill. II. Title.
PZ7.M35655Fo [E] 81-68769 AACR2
ISBN 0-8037-2668-6
ISBN 0-8037-2669-4 (lib. bdg.)

The art for each picture consists of a black ink
line-drawing with three pencil overlays reproduced
in black, red, and green halftone.

Reading Level 1.8

FOX IN TROUBLE

"Fox, dear," said Fox's mom.

"Just where do you think
you are going?"

"Out to have fun with the gang,"
said Fox.

"It's Saturday."

"But today you must take care of
little Louise," said Mom.

"You're joking," said Fox.

"I am *not* joking!" said Mom.

And she gave Fox a look.

"Come on, Louise," said Fox.

Fox went to see his friend Dexter.

But Dexter's mom came to the door.

"Sorry, Fox," she said.

"Dexter has to help at home all day."

"That's no fun," said Fox.

"Come on, Louise."

Dexter watched from the window.

"Sorry, Fox," he said.

Next Fox went to Betty's house.
"Betty has chicken pox,"
said her mom.

"Can she still play?" asked Fox.
"Of course not," said Betty's mom.

"Poor Betty," said Fox.

"Come on, Louise."

"Okay," said Louise.

"Sorry, Fox," said Betty.

"You can't help it," said Fox.

Fox went to the park

and sat down on a bench.

"This is awful!" he said.

"Today is Saturday.

But there is no one

to have fun with.

No one at all."

Fox thought long and hard.

"Nothing to do here," he said.

"Come on, Louise."

But Louise did not answer.

"She must be hiding," said Fox.

And he looked around.

But Louise was not there.

"This is serious," said Fox.

Then he looked all over the park.

Louise was gone.

"Oh, dear," said Fox.

"This is *very* serious."

Fox left the park.

"Mom will be really mad.

I have lost Louise!"

"Yoo-hoo," said a voice.

Fox looked up.

It was Louise.

"Come down this minute,"
said Fox.

"Come and get me," said Louise.

"Come down right *now*!"
said Fox.

"No!" said Louise.

"All right," said Fox.

"I'm coming up!"

Fox took a deep breath
and climbed the telephone pole.

"I don't like high places," he said.

Fox and Louise came down
the telephone pole together.

"You are trouble," said Fox.

On the way home

Fox had a terrible thought.

"What if Louise tells?"

he said to himself.

"I will really get it!"

Fox bought Louise the biggest
ice cream cone he could buy.

"You must not tell," he said.
"Maybe I will and maybe I won't,"
said Louise.

"What have you two been up to?"
asked Mom.

Fox held his breath.

"We went to the park," said Louise.

"And?" said Mom.

"And Fox bought me

an ice cream cone," said Louise.

"And?" said Mom.

"And then we came home,"
said Louise.

"How sweet, Fox," said Mom.

"You're okay, Louise," said Fox.

FOX
ALL WET

When Fox got home
from school,
Mom had a surprise for him.
"This afternoon
you must take care of Louise,"
she said.

"You're joking," said Fox.
"I'm going swimming
with my friends."
"Then you will take Louise,"
said Mom.

"No," said Fox.

Mom gave Fox a serious look.
"You will take Louise,"
she said.

"Get your suit, Louise," said Fox.
"Okay," said Louise.

At the pool Fox met his friends
Dexter, Carmen, and Junior.
"Hi!" said Fox.

"Who's the kid?" asked Carmen.
"Don't mind her," said Fox.

"Last one in the pool

is a monkey's uncle!" said Dexter.

And everyone ran for the pool.

Soon everyone was having a lot of fun.

"This is wild!" said Fox.

And everyone agreed.

"Who will jump from
the high board?" said Dexter.
"Not I," said Carmen.
"Not I," said Junior.

"I don't like high places,"
said Fox.

"Where's that kid?" asked Carmen.

"Uh-oh," said Fox.

"How did she get up there?"
asked Dexter.

"We weren't watching,"
said Carmen.

"Come down right *now*!"
said Fox.

"Come and get me,"
said Louise.

"You'll be sorry
when I do!" said Fox.

Fox climbed up the ladder.
"I don't like this at all,"
he said.

He felt his knees begin to shake.
"Don't look down,"
said Dexter.

But when Fox got to the top,

Louise was not there.

"Uh-oh," said Fox.

He felt all funny inside.

"Go on and jump!" said Dexter.

"The kid did it," said Carmen.

"Jump!" said Junior and Louise.

"Everyone is watching!" said Fox.

"We're waiting!" said Dexter.

"It's now or never," said Fox.

He closed his eyes.

And he jumped.

Fox hit with a big splash.

"Hooray for Fox!" everyone cried.

"What a fine jump!"

"Louise," said Fox. "I want to speak with you alone."

FOX
ON DUTY

Fox liked being

on traffic patrol.

His job was helping folks

across the street.

He did it very well.

Every day Fox helped
an old dog to cross.
"Thank you, Fox,"
said the old dog.
"I couldn't do it without you."

One day Fox's friends
Dexter and Carmen
stopped by his corner.

"What a dumb way
to spend your time,"
said Dexter.

"We are going swimming
at the beach,"
said Carmen.

"That sounds like fun,"
said Fox.
"Come with us," said Dexter.

"But I don't have a suit," said Fox.

"That's okay," said his friends.

"We won't look."

So Fox put down his sign

and went with his friends.

At the beach

Fox and his friends

had just as much fun as always.

They rode the waves,

and they built castles

in the sand.

Dexter and Carmen
went for hot dogs.
And Fox lay down
in the sand.

Very soon
he was dreaming away.

In his dream

Fox saw a corner, his corner.

And the sidewalk was full

of old dogs.

Some of them

could not see very well.

"I can't understand it,"
said one old dog.
"Fox is always
on duty here."
"The traffic is so heavy today,"
said another.

"We will just have to
cross the street alone,"
said the first old dog.
"There is nothing else to do."
So all the old dogs
stepped off the sidewalk.

"No!" cried Fox. "Not that!"

And he woke right up.

He did not wait for

Dexter and Carmen.

He left the beach

in a flash.

There was only one old dog
on the sidewalk.

And he was cross.

"Where were *you*?" he said.

"It won't happen again,"

said Fox.

And he helped the old dog
across the street.

"Thanks," said the dog.

"Any time," said Fox.

"And, Fox," said the old dog.

"Yes?" said Fox.

"Next time," said the dog,

"you should wear some clothes."

"Uh-oh," said Fox.